LARRY -

Motive for Murder

JEFF MARKOWITZ

ISBN: 9798470969798

To Randall, Jasmine,

Tony, Aadhik, Cooper and Bonnie.

ACKNOWLEDGMENTS

I want to thank Good Shepherd Services for inviting me to write a novella that would blur the lines between fiction and reality and would serve as the framework for Compass 2021.

Compass is an "epic late night puzzle hunt in the streets of New York City." Teams of six "hunt for, contemplate, unravel, decipher, and ultimately solve a series of unique puzzles embedded in the urban landscape of New York City."

This bi-annual event raises funds to support non-profit services to over 30,000 at-risk children and families in NYC, through the efforts of Good Shepherd Services.

I wrote the novella specifically for Compass, but I believe that *Motive for Murder* is a damn good story that stands on its own. I hope you enjoy it.

THE POSTCARD

Absent-mindedly, Randall sorted through the remaining mail. A postcard fluttered to the floor. When he bent over to pick it up, he could hear his lower back complain. An old rowing injury. He stared at the card. "REMINDER," the postcard said, in all caps, "YOUR PRESENCE IS REQUIRED AT 2:00, OCTOBER 16." Just that, and no more, except for a meeting location.

Randall didn't recognize the address and didn't remember scheduling a meeting. He quickly googled the location. It appeared to be a midtown office building, one of a thousand such buildings, except there were no owners or tenant listings, no phone numbers, no identifying information. Given more time, he was certain he could sort it out, but after allowing the postcard to sit unread for two days, his time had run out. It was October 16. He checked his watch. 2:30.

His presence was required. Most men would have ignored the summons, but Randall Riggs Jr. was not most men. He had long ago learned the importance of showing up. He thought back to his freshman year at Princeton, mandatory attendance at Economics 101. He would have aced the class, only every three absences cost one letter grade. Randall got a C.

Randall was a man defined by his routines. Every day, when he got home, he chatted with the doorman and then picked up his mail from the building's cluster mailbox. He took the elevator to his apartment on the fifth floor and put the mail in quarantine.

Approaching his thirty-third birthday, Randall worked out just enough to keep his back pain under control. He had good skin, great hair and wore the same size he had at Princeton. He lived alone in a two bedroom apartment not far from Central Park, with a spacious kitchen, and a brick fireplace.

Randall understood that there was no need to quarantine the mail. Those days, thankfully, were just about over. But after quarantining all incoming mail for more than a year, it had become part of his daily routine. After two days in quarantine, Randall would open and read the mail. He never worried about the delay. If it was important, he reasoned, they wouldn't deliver it by mail.

Randall sorted through a small stack of two-day old junk mail. Nothing of any importance, Randall noted, a receipt from a recent purchase (one of those long-thin receipts that seemed to go on forever), a Valpak (Randall quickly thumbed through the coupons, looking for any he might use) and a notice from building management about a proposed increase in the rental charge. His parents would undoubtedly say something about the rent, they might even threaten to stop paying, lecturing him about adult responsibilities, but that would get pushed off to some far-distant date and then forgotten, just as it had in the past.

Randall knew that his parents would continue to supplement his salary. And why not? They could afford it. He thought of their financial support like compensation. After all, he had to go through life as Randall Riggs Jr.

***

The subway would be the fastest way to get to the meeting, but Randall opted for a rideshare. It was a quarter past three when he was buzzed into the building on 7th Avenue, between 27th and 28th Street. Narrow hallways, dirty carpets, the slightly sweet scent of urine, elevators in need of repair – just another day in the business capital of the free world. Randall wondered whether his father might be the building's owner. He found his way to the fourth floor office.

Just inside the entrance, a reception desk sat, unattended. A row of cubicles lined one wall. The central space was sparsely furnished, one large conference table in the middle of the room and a stack of office chairs tilting dangerously toward four individuals sitting at the table. Randall examined the four closely. He knew them all from work, but not all equally well.

First was Tony, an older man, with wrinkles etched deeply in a once handsome face, wearing khaki slacks, his trademark brightly colored sweater. Tony worked in the corporate office on Fifth Avenue. Randall didn't deal with Tony routinely, but whenever they'd had cause to interact, Randall had been impressed by the man's abilities. Next to Tony sat Aadhik, an Indian gentleman with olive skin, wearing a black business suit and silk paisley tie. Aadhik, like Tony, worked out of the corporate office. Randall didn't know much about Aadhik. Rounding out the group were Cooper and Bonnie. Like Randall, Cooper and Bonnie had office space in the company's satellite office, but for the past year, had mostly worked from home. Cooper was wearing knee-length shorts and a golf shirt, his club's insignia stitched on the pocket. It seemed that every shirt Cooper owned had his club insignia stitched on the pocket. Bonnie could pass for Randall's sister, a little older, perhaps a little heavier, but unmistakably another him. Except that Bonnie proudly wore Harvard Crimson. She tipped her Harvard Crimson cap at Randall when he arrived. Bonnie found that funny, but Randall was not amused. Randall didn't remember why they had agreed to such a meeting. Perhaps his memory was playing tricks.

A lone man paced. The pacer turned to face Randall.

"You're late."

Randall didn't recognize the office, or the man who spoke to him. Something about the place (and the person) made him shiver. "I just got the postcard an hour ago."

"Cut the crap, Randall." The man grinned, exposing the teeth of a carnivore. "Get a chair and sit down. I believe you know Tony, Aadhik, Cooper and Bonnie."

Randall stared, a little too obviously at the one empty chair at the table. The carnivore licked his lips. "That one's already spoken for."

Randall examined the stacking chairs. He couldn't reach the top of the stack. And he couldn't safely remove a chair from the bottom. "I'll stand."

"Suit yourself," the carnivore said, grinning ear-to-ear.

Randall was growing impatient. He had, he told himself, been more than accommodating, dropping everything to be here. Beyond the address, he still didn't know where here was.

Just then, the office door flew open. Randall's breathing quickened. His face flushed. A young woman with long blond hair wearing a hippie dress and sandals sashayed into the office. Randall stared at the mysterious stranger, wondering who she was and why she was there. Why any of them were there. Without saying a word, she lay claim to the universe and everything in it.

"I'm here," Jasmine warbled.

"I saved you a seat," Randall stammered, pointing to the table.

"Thank you sweetie." She gave Randall her hand.

He didn't know what he was expected to do with her hand. Red-faced, he escorted her to the one empty chair. "What's this about, anyway?"

The carnivore grinned. "A Motive for Murder."

The color drained from Randall's face. He looked around the room, as if the nondescript office might hold some clue. He waited for the carnivore to continue.

"Now that I've got your attention… I'm the agent who gets to decide whether or not you get sent to the big show… whether you get what you deserve. So don't waste my time, don't feed me some line. I have no doubt that one of you had the lead role in this and all of you played some part."

"I don't think I'm supposed to be here." Randall started backing toward the exit.

"Sit down and shut up. I'm doing you a favor. Later you're going to have to answer to a higher authority." The carnivore paused. "So let's start over. Who knows why you're all here in my office?"

Randall shrugged. "Not me."

"Stop pretending that you don't know what happened."

Jasmine stepped between Randall and the carnivore. "If he says he doesn't know, then he doesn't know."

The carnivore looked around the room. "Who can tell me when this went down?"

Jasmine smiled innocently, one bright spot in an otherwise dismal afternoon. "When what happened?"

"Okay, where did it happen then?" The carnivore pointed at Cooper. "You!"

Cooper stared at his hands and said nothing.

The carnivore tried to control his rising anger. "Someone is going to tell me about the victim." He approached Aadhik. "I want details."

But Aadhik had no details to offer. "I'm sorry sir, but I don't know what you're talking about."

The carnivore was losing his patience. "What was the victim wearing?"

Bonnie sighed. "If we don't know the victim, how could we possibly know what he was wearing?"

"Did the victim have anything unusual? Money? Jewelry? Drugs?"

Tony tried to defuse the situation. "We'd like to be more helpful, but it should be obvious by now that you're talking to the wrong people."

The carnivore banged his fist on the table. "You're all going to have to account for your whereabouts when this was happening." He looked around at the gang of six. "Who wants to go first?"

There was an uneasy silence in the room.

The carnivore was growing impatient. "Randall... Jasmine, stay here. The rest of you can go."

Tony looked at Randall. "It's okay. We'll wait for you downstairs." Tony walked to the exit. Aadhik, Cooper and Bonnie followed, without saying a word.

The carnivore pointed at the cubicle. "In there." He followed Randall into the cubicle. To Randall, it felt like the carnivore was stalking his prey. And he was the prey. He should at least know the name of the man who was on his trail.

"Who are you?"

The carnivore grinned. "My friends call me Benny."

Randall wondered about the carnivore's notion of friendship.

The cubicle was empty.

The carnivore continued questioning Randall, probing questions about his whereabouts, his availability, and his familiarity with Murder. It was all too much. Randall exited the cubicle, dark thoughts pressing down on him. He had the beginning of a migraine headache. And his lower back hurt like a bitch. Randall made his way quickly toward the exit, but that would leave Jasmine alone with the carnivore who had started salivating again.

"Wait for me," she whispered. "Please."

THE GANG OF SIX

When Jasmine moved to Manhattan, her plan had been to become an Influencer. She would wear the coolest outfits, attend the hottest events, hobnob with the right people, post a few questionable videos, and build up her followers. Then she would sit back and watch the money roll in.

Things had not panned out. She had survived by working odd jobs. Then the virus happened and the jobs that remained were too odd, even for Jasmine.

If there had been one positive about the pandemic, it was the glut of available rental properties. Jasmine could never have afforded a studio apartment in the West Village at pre-pandemic prices, but at the height of the crisis, she signed a 12 month lease for $1500/month. It was a great price for the tiny studio, but even at $1500, it strained her budget. Everyone said that NYC was coming back strong, and maybe it was, Jasmine told herself, probably it was, but if it didn't come back quickly, even at $1500, her rent was going to become a problem. She was already a month behind, and tap dancing around the issue with her landlady.

Somehow that had led her to this moment, caught up in a mysterious interrogation with a group of strangers. If she were inclined to worry, this was surely something to worry about. She wished she could head back to her apartment and meditate.

***

When Jasmine emerged from the cubicle, she was pleased to see that Randall had, indeed, waited. She threw her arms around him, an expression of heartfelt appreciation, and perhaps a bit more. Randall was unused to being on the receiving end of hugs from uninhibited women. For Randall, the hug was one more puzzle, in a decidedly puzzling day.

"Are you okay?' Randall asked.

"I'm fabulous." Jasmine beamed. Don't you think I'm fabulous?"

Randall didn't know what to think. "What was that all about?"

"In there? I'm not sure." Jasmine chuckled. "I try not to worry about things."

"But..."

"No. No buts. Let's get out of here."

When they left the office, they found Tony, Aadhik, Cooper and Bonnie standing on the sidewalk, discussing their next move.

"This is crazy!" As he spoke, Cooper pounded on the sidewalk newspaper box for emphasis. The door popped open dispensing one copy of the Post.

"Holy crap!" Randall pointed excitedly.

They all looked at the front page story. An unidentified body had been found in a bar on E 54th Street.

Bonnie studied the newspaper, looking for more details. As she read the paper, a leaflet fell from between the pages. An advertisement for an upcoming author talk. Under other circumstances, she might have found that of interest, but for the moment her attention was focused on the news account of the recent murder.

"I know that bar. It's the French Bistro, Papillon."

According to the police, a witness reported seeing four men and two women exiting the crime scene. The newspaper was already calling them the "gang of six."

Tony's eyes popped at the reference. "Do you think… is it possible?"

Jasmine was confused. "But we've never been there." She looked at the others. "At least not all of us, together."

Aadhik nodded. "Before today, we've never been anywhere, all together."

"And yet… someone was murdered. Four men and two women may have been involved."

Randall didn't know what to believe. "It must be a coincidence."

Tony shrugged. "I don't believe in coincidence."

"Neither do I." Randall looked at the others.

They began to walk, saying nothing, each lost in their own thoughts, paying little attention to the passage of time. The city seemed unnaturally quiet.

Suddenly, the quiet was broken by a police car. The air was pierced by static from the police radio. They were close enough to hear the report. Something about a commotion at Papillon.

"I don't know about the rest, of you," Jasmine said, "but I'm starving."

Randall quickly agreed. They would think more clearly on a full stomach.

Jasmine smiled. "I know a place."

THE DUMPLING SHOP

Jasmine belonged to a Buddhist temple in Queens. The temple looked like a traditional Japanese pagoda, constructed of wood, brick and stone, with a tiered roof that was visible from the elevated subway line. She loved the little temple in Flushing, but she had grown tired of the long subway ride and all that the subway ride entailed. She opted instead to conduct daily rituals in her apartment and to attend a small, informal prayer group that met in a dumpling shop on W. 23rd St.

Jasmine was pleased that the others had agreed to stop for dumplings. It might not help them solve the puzzle, but it would fill their stomachs and soothe their troubled souls.

Several regular members of the prayer group were there, enjoying the dumplings. Jasmine pressed her hands together in front of her chest.

They put down their bowls, pressed their hands together and bid welcome to Jasmine and her guests.

Jasmine's diet prevented her from partaking of the dumplings. She never bothered to ask whether they made gluten-free vegan dumplings. It seemed to Jasmine that there was nothing more quintessentially Buddhist than to not eat dumplings in the best dumpling shop in the city.

The waiter brought out five small servings of dumplings. "And what about you, my dear. What would you like today?"

Jasmine smiled. "Could I trouble you for a plate of edamame?"

"I'll be right back." The old man moved slowly, but with purpose and returned with the edamame and a large stack of napkins.

The waiter smiled. "For you."

***

"The essential challenge to the serious Buddhist, is to achieve enlightenment, release from the cycle of death and rebirth. But for some Buddhists, the goal is not individual enlightenment, but universal enlightenment. These Buddhists believe that there are special individuals... bodhisattvas... who have achieved individual enlightenment, but who choose to remain in the world, helping the rest of us on the spiritual path." The elderly monk nodded at the men and women sitting around the table at the dumpling shop. When the group had formed, Master Chinshu agreed to assist them on their spiritual journey. He didn't like being called Master; nevertheless he accepted them as his disciples. Once a month, he travelled by subway, from Flushing into Manhattan to share a bowl of dumplings with the group. They would find enlightenment by chanting Daimoku. Until then, Master Chinshu entertained them with his lessons.

"Gradually, more and more people will get the message (that there is no message). Soon there will be more and more bodhisattvas wandering the earth, helping an ever smaller number who still haven't figured it out. Eventually we all get there, but there has to be a moment when there's just one unenlightened slob left, one guy who just doesn't get it, one loser who is standing in the way of universal enlightenment. And that hold-out, he's what I like to call the last bodhisattva, 'cause after he gets it, there's no one left to help."

Master Chinshu had been building to this point for months. Jasmine listened earnestly and patted herself on the back for she understood the lesson… that they were the bodhisattvas, small in number now, but growing every day, the spiritual leaders, at the head of the parade.

"Only sometimes I get to wondering..." she was startled, believing that the Master had completed his lesson… "if we can really trust the bodhisattvas."

He had scarcely gotten the final words out when pandemonium broke loose in the dumpling shop. Everyone had something to say; they were jumping up and down, arms and opinions akimbo, and everyone chattering away all at one time. Gradually, out of the chaos, coherent thoughts began to emerge.

"I think the point is there's good and evil in all of us," opined an older woman in the prayer group.

"That's bullshit and you know it." Jasmine had heard enough. "The retreat from absolute values is merely an excuse for evil."

No one lacked for an opinion or the willingness to share it. "I'm not sure it's that easy. I read a poem recently... I forget who wrote it... anyway he compared the dharma to an onion. You peel away layers and keep peeling until you discover the nothingness at the center of the onion."

"It was Snyder," suggested another member of the group, "and it was an avocado, not an onion. The dharma is like the pit of an avocado...hard, and just when you think you grasp it, it slips away."

It was time for the "gang of six" to slip away.

SHORT RIBS

Bonnie suggested they should head to Papillon, perhaps they could learn something about the murder.

When they got to 54th Street, a television crew was on the sidewalk, partially blocking the imposing two-story columned entrance to the bistro. Inside, the bar was busy.

They had no specific plan, but when they entered the bistro, they discovered that they didn't need a plan. They just needed to ask. Bar staff were more than happy to direct customers to the second floor crime scene.

The unresolved murder was attracting tourists, so the bar had made the decision not to remove the two-week old crime scene tape. Inside the tape, several footsteps were still visible on the bar room floor.

A waiter walked past carrying a tray of short ribs. Jasmine had been wrong on one count. The dumplings had not filled their stomachs.

Randall was salivating with anticipation. "Finally, a proper meal." He looked at Jasmine and quickly added, "The dumplings were a delightful first course, but a real man needs his meat."

Jasmine's face grew pale. "I can't eat here! I'm a gluten-free protovegan."

Randall didn't know what a protovegan was, but he was pretty sure they didn't eat short ribs. "Well, let's sit down and take a look at the menu. I'm sure you'll find something." He touched her lightly on the arm, guiding her toward their table. "My treat."

They all sat down and studied the menu. A waitress materialized at tableside. "You want to order dinner, yes?"

Jasmine felt an affinity for waitresses, for all service personnel. She made it a point to see the waitress as a unique individual. She looked at the fortyish woman waiting to take her order, the pain of standing all day apparent on her overly made-up face. Even her hair looked tired. Jasmine felt sorry for the prematurely gray lady with the crazy eyes and the aching feet.

"I'm vegan," she explained. "What do you recommend?"

"I recommend another restaurant." The waitress laughed. It was the laugh of a heavy smoker. "Actually we get positive reviews for our salads."

Jasmine checked the menu. The salads did look good, but they all seemed to have cheese or croutons. "Can you bring me a kale salad," she asked, "without the ricotto salata?"

"Good choice, ma'am. And you sir?" She looked at Randall.

"Is the short rib sandwich good?"

The waitress smiled. "It's one of our most popular items."

"Excellent. I'll have the sandwich with a side of truffle fries." He handed the menu to the waitress.

The rest of the table ordered their entrees. The waitress filled their water glasses and brought them a basket of bread. Randall offered the basket to Jasmine, but she waved him off. "I don't eat bread."

"I can't keep up with all those fad diets."

"Eating healthy is not a fad. Our bodies were designed to be vegan. Meat is the fad."

"If you say so. Still, you have to admit, if meat is a fad, it's been a fad now for thousands of years."

"Perhaps." Jasmine wasn't in the mood for an argument. She excused herself and went off in search of the ladies' room.

Bonnie jumped to her feet. "Excuse me, gentlemen." She hurried off after Jasmine.

In the privacy of the ladies' room, Bonnie got straight to the point. "I don't have anything to do with that murder. And you?" You don't look like the murdering type." Bonnie held her breath, waiting for Jasmine's answer.

"Of course not." Jasmine smiled shyly. "I'm opposed to violence of any kind."

Bonnie exhaled. "I'm glad. Still…" Bonnie was not prepared to dismiss the carnivore's suspicions completely. "What did he want from you?"

Jasmine wasn't sure what to say. She decided to settle on the truth. "He asked me about this place. I told him I'd never been here."

"Do you think one of the men could be involved."

"No." Jasmine fiddled with small prayer beads that she wore on her wrist. "I don't think so."

By unspoken agreement, the four men waited until the ladies returned and finished their meals before returning to the subject of murder.

At the mention of murder, their waitress, hustling back with one herbal tea, five coffees and a small bowl of French cream, stopped dead in her tracks. For just a moment, suspended in time, everything simply stopped. Everything, that is, except for the cream, which, obeying the immutable laws of inertial motion continued along its forward trajectory, landing, with eerie accuracy in Jasmine's army surplus rucksack.

Jasmine sat there, quietly meditating, a serene center, waiting for the excitement to subside.

BEHIND A RED CURTAIN

It had been a long and confusing day. Randall said his goodbyes and left Papillon, alone at last. He looked forward to his apartment, to a nightcap and a good night's sleep. It was a bit of a distance, but the walk would help settle him down. He took his time strolling uptown, the moon shining brightly above Central Park. Six blocks from home, storm clouds rolled down from the north. Four blocks from home, it was raining lightly. Randall turned up his collar and picked up his pace. Two blocks from the apartment, there was a crack of thunder. Rain poured from the sky in a rush, like bullets hitting the glass and brick structures. By the time he got home, Randall was soaked.

He was in no mood to chat with the doorman. Still, it rankled him when he was absent his post. The doorman was supposed to be there. Randall had already retrieved the mail; it was the mail, after all, that had kicked off this adventure, but he stopped anyway to check his empty mailbox. No doorman and no mail. Not the way he liked to enter the apartment building. To be safe, he checked the mailbox a second time, before taking the elevator to the fifth floor.

He peeled off the soaking wet clothes, tossing them in a pile in the bathroom. He pulled on a pair of blue plaid pajama pants and an old Princeton tee-shirt and settled in front of his laptop. It had been quite a day. But what, in the end, did Randall know. Very little actually. A man named Benny (the "carnivore") had accused him of having something to do with a murder. Perhaps the same murder as the one in the newspaper. Beyond that, the details were sketchy. He didn't know the name of the victim, or the cause of death. He didn't know who wanted the man dead or why. Randall stopped himself, before moving on with an inventory of events. He didn't even know if the dead man was a man. He tried to envision a woman's body, snuggled inside the chalk outline. Most troubling of all, the reference in the newspaper to a "gang of six."

What else did Randall know? He knew that Jasmine appeared to like him. She also liked kale. Randall knew that kale was a popular super-food (whatever that meant). A few of his friends ate kale, but none of them seemed to like kale. Jasmine liked kale. Maybe that meant something. Everything meant something, he told himself. It's just hard to know what meant a lot, and what meant a very little.

Randall was good at figuring stuff out. Not useful stuff. Not stuff that other people cared about. Arcane stuff. Esoteric stuff.

He logged onto his laptop. He decided to start with the carnivore. Without a last name, his first search yielded approximately 275,000 results. Next, he tried Jasmine. That resulted in 388,000 hits. He was going to need more information. Was it possible that they knew one another? He tried googling "jasmine and benny" and threw the laptop across the room. Just shy of eighteen million results for "jasmine and benny." At least the laptop had landed on a throw pillow. No harm. No foul. And no answers.

He had a glass of scotch to take the edge off, and prepared for bed. Sipping a nightcap was his favorite routine, except, sometimes it caused the most vivid dreams...

... He climbed onto the empty elevator and pushed the lobby button. The elevator went whizzing along horizontally, accelerating all the while. The elevator took a banked hard right turn and continued to pick up speed. That's when Randall noticed the woman. She must have gotten on when the elevator stopped, but Randall knew that wasn't possible. The elevator had made no stops.

The next morning, that was all Randall could remember of his scotch-fueled dream. He lay in bed, stuck somewhere between dreaming and reality...

... Behind a red curtain, Randall found the gang of six, waiting for him. Tony, Cooper, Bonnie and Aadhik were drinking whiskey on expense accounts, paying scant attention to the dead starlet on the bar room floor. Randall held a pocket mirror to the dead woman's face. She wasn't breathing. He checked the dead woman's pulse. There was none.

Jasmine sat up and gave him a hug. She smiled at him. "I knew you'd come."

THE TILT OF HIS FEDORA

Jasmine was waiting on the sidewalk in front of the bookstore when Randall climbed out of the rideshare.

"I knew you'd come," she squealed, giving him a great big hug.

For the briefest of moments, Randall felt a wave of uneasiness, like high tide in his gastro-intestinal tract. He set both feet firmly on the pavement and gulped deeply for air.

"What are we doing here?"

Jasmine smiled indulgently. "Don't you remember? The newspaper? The unsolved murder? Surely you remember the murder?"

Randall wasn't sure whether to be angry or amused. "Of course I remember the murder. But I don't remember any mention of this place." Randall waved his hand, like a tipsy spokesmodel, at the spy museum. "Why are we here at..." Randall peered at the signage... "Spyscape?"

Jasmine smiled indulgently. "You do remember the newspaper?"

"Of course."

"There was an advertisement. According to the ad, the author talk will be here tonight, the topic is the author's new murder mystery. I have a strong feeling it might help us to understand our own murder mystery."

"Are the others here yet?"

Jasmine and Randall walked into Spyscape, looking for the other members of the gang of six. They located the bookshop on the lower level; an employee directed them to a large hall upstairs.

The hall was filled with chairs, much like the stacking chairs at the mysterious office, but more comfortable. Some of the seats were already occupied, but most of the people were milling about, chatting. At the front of the room, there was a podium.

The author turned out to be an older man, with a well-trimmed beard and a shit-eating grin. He was balding and slightly overweight. He hid the bald spot as best he could under a black fedora. The extra poundage was harder to hide.

Randall and Jasmine walked toward the front of the room. The author was reviewing his notes. He paused for the briefest of moments, to stare as Randall and Jasmine approached. Randall noticed the pause. Something about the author tugged at Randall's memory.

He picked up a copy of the book. MOTIVE FOR MURDER, in big bold letters. By Jeff Markowitz. "Is that you?"

"My friends call me Jeff."

"So you wrote this?"

"I did."

"What's it about?"

The author grinned. "It's about 100 pages."

Jasmine nudged Randall. "We should take our seats."

They barely had time to sit down before their host banged on the podium to get everyone's attention.

"Welcome," he said "to Spyscape. We're excited to have Jeff Markowitz here today to talk about his new book." He held up a copy of MOTIVE FOR MURDER. "And we're equally pleased to see so many people have joined us here today."

Randall looked around the room. All the seats were taken. He was pleased to see that Tony and Aadhik were already there. Tony, as always, wore a brightly colored sweater. Aadhik still wore his suit and silk paisley tie. Customers continued to arrive, standing along the rear wall. At the last minute, Randall noticed Bonnie and Cooper, standing in back, deep in conversation. He wondered if they knew more than he did. They would need to put their heads together if they were going to solve the puzzle. Randall sent Tony a text. Tony checked his phone, looked around the room, spotted Randall, and nodded his agreement.

"Before I turn this over to our author, I need to tell you how we're handling today's event. Jeff is going to tell us a bit about his book, and, hopefully about his writing process. He'll read a brief excerpt. Then we'll open it up to questions. When we're finished, you can go back downstairs and get your autographed copy of MOTIVE FOR MURDER. You do not want to leave here tonight without a copy of MOTIVE FOR MURDER."

The author stood in front of the room. He adjusted the tilt of his fedora and thanked everyone for coming.

"No matter how many books I write, it's always nerve-wracking when a new book is released."

A woman in the front row raised her hand. Without waiting to be recognized, she blurted out, "How many books have you written?"

The store employee smacked himself in the head. "Please hold your questions until the end."

"I'm sorry," the woman said, clearly embarrassed. "Is it part of a series or a standalone?"

The author tried, unsuccessfully, to suppress a laugh. "Perhaps it's the first book in a new series."

The store employee stared down on the offending customer. She got the message. "Please, go on."

Jeff cleared his throat. "I find dead bodies."

Randall turned toward Jasmine, but said nothing.

"I mean, anytime that people congregate in large groups, the event becomes more interesting if you discover a dead body. Think about it. A business meeting. Your high school reunion. A fundraising gala." The author chuckled, enjoying a private joke. "The point is, there are dead bodies everywhere. It's my job to find them. When I do, I jot down a sentence or two memorializing the discovery. Sometimes that sentence leads to a book."

Jeff knew that he was saying more than he should. Every writer, no matter how gifted, needs an editor.

"MOTIVE FOR MURDER will take you on a hunt, of sorts, across Manhattan, searching for the clues to solve a cold-blooded murder. I'd like to read you a brief excerpt" –

***

Absent-mindedly, Randall sorted through the remaining mail. A postcard fluttered to the floor. When he bent over to pick it up, he could hear his lower back complain. An old rowing injury. He stared at the card. "REMINDER," the postcard said, in all caps, "YOUR PRESENCE IS REQUIRED AT 2:00, OCTOBER 16." Just that, and no more, except for a meeting location.

***

Sitting in the audience, Randall was freaking out. He grabbed Jasmine by the shoulders. In a too-loud whisper, his words spewed out in a torrent.

"Holy shit! He's writing about me!" Randall shivered at the thought. "How the fuck can he be writing about me?"

"Shhh, everyone can hear you."

Randall looked around. Jasmine was right. All eyes were on him. But Randall couldn't stop. "How does he know my story? It doesn't make sense."

Randall's world was spinning out of control. Somehow, this author had written the story of his life. Jasmine was shushing him, trying to prevent him from making a scene. Meanwhile the author continued reading.

***

When they left the office, they found Tony, Aadhik, Cooper and Bonnie standing on the sidewalk, discussing their next move.

"This is crazy!" As he spoke, Cooper pounded on the sidewalk newspaper box for emphasis. The door popped open dispensing one copy of the Post.

"Holy crap!" Randall pointed excitedly.

They all looked at the front page story. An unidentified body had been found in a bar on E 54th Street.

Bonnie studied the newspaper, looking for more details. As she read the paper, a leaflet fell from between the pages. An advertisement for an upcoming author talk. Under other circumstances, she might have found that of interest, but for the moment her attention was focused on the news account of the recent murder.

"I know that bar. It's the French Bistro, Papillon."

According to the police, a witness reported seeing four men and two women exiting the crime scene. The newspaper was already calling them the "gang of six."

***

The author put the book down. "I think that's a good place to stop. Does anyone have any questions?"

Before he could finish asking, a dozen hands went up. Jeff pointed first to Randall. Randall had a million questions, but couldn't figure out how to ask any of them. After an awkward pause, the author moved on to an older man, wrinkles etched deeply in his face.

"I'm working on a book about spies in the banking industry," Tony said, "but I'm finding it difficult to settle into a writing routine. What's your process?"

"You know, I get that question all the time. I could tell you about my process, but the truth is, my process doesn't matter. What matters is that you find your own process, and once you find it, you commit to it."

"That makes sense, I guess, but what's your process?"

Jeff chuckled. "Okay. Here's the thing. I think about writing a book like taking a cross-country road trip. I know where and when I'm going to set out. I know my destination and when I intend to get there. And I know a few stops along the way. Between the planned stops, I let the journey unfold in its own way. Maybe I see a billboard for the world's largest ball of twine, so I take a detour to visit. I mean, who wouldn't want to see the world's largest ball of twine? Or the international tuba museum? I go where the story takes me. But I have to find my way back to

St. Louis on Thursday. And Denver the following Friday. If I don't make it, on time, to my intermediate stops, I won't have a book when I get to the ending." The author surveyed the room. "You, in the back. The one with the golf shirt."

Cooper stood up. "Is this a work of fiction or nonfiction?"

"That is a very good question. I like to think of it as a dramatization. You know, ripped from the headlines. So perhaps it's fair to say it's a bit of both. I have cultivated some very good sources, people who are inside the department." Jeff smiled. "But a good writer never reveals everything."

The store employee spoke up. "Does anyone else have a question for our author?"

Aadhik had a question.

"Are you familiar with the city's Hall of Records? Is it open to the general public?"

The author smiled. This one could be a problem. Before he could answer, the store employee jumped back in.

"I think that's a good place to stop," the store employee said. Let's give Jeff a moment to catch his breath, and then he'll sign your books."

A GOOD SIDE

"That was weird." Randall was still in shock from the unfolding of events at the book signing.

When they left the bookstore, the "gang of six" retreated to a falafel joint a couple of blocks from the spy museum. Randall had wanted to retreat to his apartment, alone, where he intended to freak out more privately. Jasmine sat across from Randall, trying to de-compress. She breathed in deeply through her nose and exhaled slowly through her mouth. It seemed to Randall that Jasmine wasn't upset enough. After all, her life story, also, would be revealed in the author's book.

"Doesn't it bother you?"

Jasmine exhaled. "It would, if I let it."

"How do you not let it?" Randal's voice was getting louder. In the nearly empty shop, the few other customers turned to stare. Randall reined in his panic, as best he could. His best, given the situation was not good enough.

"Am I losing my mind? Randall picked up the pilsner glass and took a long swig of Goldstar. "I feel like we landed in the middle of a Twilight Zone episode."

"Maybe we did. I don't want to get all metaphysical on you, but what is reality anyway?"

Randall didn't know how to answer. Until the day that postcard arrived, Randall thought he knew the difference between reality and fiction. Now he wasn't so sure. He sipped his beer. "Maybe I don't know what reality is, but I sure as hell know what it's not. It's not finding a barely disguised version of yourself in someone's book." Randall looked around the table, hoping to find agreement. He took a deep breath and pushed ahead. "We should sue his ass for defamation of character."

"Perhaps you're looking at this the wrong way." Jasmine shook her head. "Perhaps there's a good side to all this."

"A good side!" Randall was ready to explode.

Jasmine chuckled softly. "There's always a good side."

Aadhik nodded. "I think what Jasmine means is, perhaps the author can help us."

Randall had already had enough. The last thing he wanted was any more help from the author.

Jasmine tried her best to explain. "But if the author has information that could help us prove our innocence, then we owe it to ourselves to find out."

Tony had a suggestion. "Maybe we don't need the author. Maybe we can find what we need in his book."

"I guess you're right." Randall agreed, grudgingly. "But the guy creeps me out."

"Well, yes, he is a little creepy." Jasmine smiled sweetly.

Randall was still trying to connect the dots, in his head. The last couple of days had been more than he could process. The nearly empty office building, the interrogation, the carnivore, the newspaper story, the implication that they were somehow complicit in an as yet unsolved murder, and now, of course, their appearance in Jeff's book. There was a big difference between solving a mystery and being the mystery. They had a lot to figure out, but the more Randall listened to Jasmine, the more, at least for the moment, her serenity seemed to rub off on them.

"I notice, sometimes, when you're agitated, you chant. Does that help?"

"Why don't you give it a try? Repeat after me, 'Nam-myoho-renge kyo'."

Randall felt foolish. "Mam-myoho-renge-kyo?"

"Almost." Jasmine and Randall were both laughing.

All six of them began chanting. "Nam-myoho-renge-kyo." The anxiety was washing away, like lily pads caught in a swiftly flowing stream.

"Don't you feel better now?"

Much to their surprise, they agreed that they did.

Randall told himself he was going to be okay. He walked over to the counter to order a second beer.

POLICE BLOTTER

After the book signing, Randall and Tony continued to exchange texts, cautiously sharing information. Randall figured that just because the carnivore was wrong about his involvement, didn't mean that he was wrong about everyone's involvement in the mysterious murder case. Tony apparently was thinking the same thing. They both wanted to solve the mystery, only neither could be certain of the other's innocence. Ultimately they came to the realization that they had to stem the growing distrust that festered among the gang of six. Their only hope was to trust each other. Tony offered to host a meeting at the corporate office. He ushered them into his conference room, a large mahogany table, six high-back brown leather chairs, an elaborate single-brew coffee service laid out on a side table. Randall took one look at the coffee service and groaned. The same self-satisfied coffee that was sweeping Manhattan. Served with non-dairy creamer and a choice of sugar substitutes.

For the first fifteen minutes, the four men and two women spoke mostly about their anxiety (and a little bit about Cooper's football pool). No one seemed comfortable sharing what they knew or suspected about the interrogation. Randall began to think that calling the meeting had been a waste of time.

Then Aadhik stood up. "I have something to say."

"When I was a youngster, I liked to read the police blotter. It was like reading Page Six, only it came with the imprimatur of the NYPD. As I got older, I lost interest. But when I left the interrogation, I decided to see what I could find. Of course, those records are available online these days. Not only does it make searching easier, but you don't get newsprint on your hands. I found something interesting just this morning."

Aadhik paused, for dramatic effect, fixing the knot on his silk paisley tie.

"C'mon Aadhik, this isn't some stage play. What did you find?"

Aadhik insisted on making himself a cup of coffee before he would continue.

"Two weeks before we were summoned to the interrogation, a body was found in Papillon."

Cooper was growing impatient. "We ALL saw the crime scene. Did you find out anything we don't already know? Anything about the dead man's identity?"

Jasmine jumped into the conversation. "I think it was a dead woman."

"Why do you say that?"

"When we were at the crime scene, I got a vision of a dead woman."

"Maybe. The newspaper account didn't reveal any details about the victim."

"No," Jasmine admitted. "But I've learned to trust my visions."

All four men, and two women, were talking all at the same time. Aadhik had to raise his voice to be heard over the din. "Jasmine is right. It was a dead woman, with bright red hair and a stab wound above her left breast, a rust-colored blood stain on her pale green dress."

Cooper was skeptical. "You got all that from the police blotter?"

Aadhik grinned. "From the police blotter, yes, but not just the police blotter. Once I had the basics, I started hunting. One clue led to the next, until, this morning, I made a visit to the Hall of Records, where it all started to come together. According to a report in the Hall of Records, the dead woman was found with a folder crammed full of documents about the building where Papillon is located."

Tony rubbed his head. "Did you find the dead woman's name?"

"Sadly, no. Either her identity was unknown to the authorities, or perhaps merely undisclosed." Aadhik shook his head and reached into his pocket. "But I did find a picture."

Aadhik passed it to Jasmine, sitting to his right. "I must warn you. If you haven't seen an autopsy photo before, it can be pretty unsettling."

When Jasmine looked at the photo, she nearly threw up. She had seen that red hair before. Jasmine struggled to regain her composure. When the time was right, she would tell them what she suspected.

Tony reached for the photo.

Cooper started to say something, but thought better of it.

Tony spoke up. “At least we have a place to start. Would anyone like to suggest a next step?”

Randall looked up. “I may be able to reach out to someone.”

Aadhik assumed Randall had a friend on the force. “Is it safe to talk to someone in law enforcement?”

“Not law enforcement.” Randall cringed at what he was about to suggest. “Building management.”

RIGGS & SON

Someone had to own the building. And someone had to handle the building operations. There were a limited number of real estate management companies likely to have an interest in the building. Randall's father owned one of them. Randall plugged in the web address for Riggs & Son Royal Management. He got angry typing in the company name. Most people assumed, incorrectly, that Randall Senior and Junior were Riggs & Son. They were off by a generation.

The Riggs that was referred to in the company name was Randall's late grandfather Edmund Riggs. The company had been a major player in NYC real estate starting in the 1930s as the city began to build itself out of the Great Depression. Edmund made a fortune in NYC real estate and groomed his son, Randall Sr. to follow in his footsteps. Randall Sr. inherited his father's substantial investment portfolio, and his skill, but not his passion for real estate. The company made money anyway, real estate in the city, for all intents and purposes, selling itself.

Randall Sr. didn't like selling real estate, but he did like having his name on some prime properties. And he liked supplanting his father and becoming the Riggs in Riggs & Son. Of course, that meant Randall Jr. would have to join the family business. Hard as Sr. tried, he couldn't warm up to his son and he couldn't understand why that mattered. They were family. That should have been enough.

Of course, it wasn't enough. Randall Jr. assumed that there would come a day, when his father was dead, that he would inherit the company. Until then, he had no interest in actively joining the family business. Sr. secretly was relieved that his son would not replace him as he had replaced his own father. Without the bonds of family or business keeping them together, father and son grew apart. After the car accident, they stopped talking completely.

Over time, the brand's luster, just like the family's, was tarnished. The building on E. 54th Street, was just the sort of project that might be of interest to Riggs & Son.

There was nothing in the public pages on the company website that made mention of the bar or the building on E. 54th Street. But the website had a secure section, not available to the general public.

Randall poured himself a second cup of coffee and set about the task of accessing the company's records. Once upon a time, when they were both younger, his father had established an email account for Jr. in hopes that he would take an interest in the business. Much to his surprise, his email was still active, his password unchanged.

He was almost in. It seems that his father had created a second level of security. He made a guess about his father's likely password, and let the computer process thousands of combinations and permutations. Before he finished the second cup of coffee, the computer had hit upon the correct variation.

He scrolled through the secure pages on his father's website. He didn't have the time or the patience to read everything, but he bookmarked a couple of potentially interesting stories, before studying the list of the company's current projects. Riggs & Son didn't manage the property on E. 54th Street. But Randall was convinced that there was a connection. He could feel it. Now he just had to find it. He clicked on the link to archived records. That's when Randall hit paydirt. Riggs & Son had managed the property until 2005.

***

Randall sat down in a booth at P. Dello's, a café on the ground floor of the Rodman Edward Building. Riggs & Son occupied the sixth floor. He tried to remember the last time he'd been there. He counted backwards through a litany of family disputes. It had been ten years, he concluded, since he last saw his father. He sipped the coffee slowly. Let it be ten years and fifteen minutes. A second cup of bad coffee would not make things any easier. He paid for the coffee, leaving the waitress a sizable tip, and walked purposefully down the hall to the elevator.

A fortyish year-old woman in a pearl gray dress climbed on with him. "Could you push six, please" she asked. Randall took a closer look. The dress was stylish, but business-like, the cleavage perhaps a bit too revealing, but Randall was no expert on business attire. She'd had some work done. Not too much, Randall noted, just enough to shave a few years off her resume.

When they climbed off the elevator, Randall held the door open for her. "Have a nice day."

They nodded their goodbyes and then laughed when they realized they were heading for the same destination. Randall held the door open again when they got to the office that housed Riggs & Son. She thanked him for his courtesy and sat down behind the reception desk.

"Can I help you?"

Somehow he had expected to find Molly sitting at reception. "I'm here to see Mr. Riggs."

"Do you have an appointment?" She smiled sweetly and opened her calendar.

"No." Randall wasn't sure what to say next. "I'm his son."

The receptionist's eyes brightened. "I'm sorry. I didn't realize." She snuck a peek at Randall's hand. No wedding ring. "I'll buzz Mr. Riggs' personal assistant."

Before Randall had time to think, an inner door swung slowly open. From behind the half-open door, Molly O'Sullivan peeked into the lobby. She put on a smile. "It's good to see you, Randall."

"You too, Molly," his face flushed.

"It's been a long time." Molly gave him the once-over. "How are you?"

"I'm good."

"Come on back. There's a lot to talk about."

"My father?"

"He's out."

"Okay then."

Molly started to show him the way, but even after a decade, Randall knew his way around Riggs & Son.

"So you're the old man's personal assistant now."

Molly didn't know what to say. "Your father never blamed me."

Randall shook his head in disgust. "He blamed me."

"It was," Molly said, trying to keep her voice steady, "your fault."

They sat on the sofa in Molly's office and stared at one another, lost in their thoughts. Molly remembered the boy she had once been in love with. Randall remembered nothing but the break-up.

They were barely out of college then, Randall in Manhattan, and Molly with a job in Ohio. She told him she couldn't come to New York for the holidays. She was working on an important project with a tight deadline. He desperately wanted to see her, to set things right between them. It might have occurred to him that the project was an excuse, that the reason he needed to apologize was the same reason she didn't want to see him. But he didn't. He borrowed his father's luxury sedan and drove eight hours straight, arriving at Molly's doorstep in time for dinner.

They spoke through the closed door, the conversation brutally civil. He could still remember every muffled word.

He had driven eight hours non-stop, and arrived in time for a heart wrenching breakup. Randall should have spent the night in a highway motel, but he wanted to get as far away from Cleveland as his father's automobile could take him. Randall got back in the car, heading east. Before he got out of Ohio, It started to snow. Halfway between Cleveland and Manhattan, he hit an icy patch on Interstate 80 and flipped his father's luxury sedan.

Randall was hanging upside-down, strapped inside the crushed vehicle, when Molly's question drew him back to Riggs & Son.

"What are you doing here?"

"Here?" Randall looked around, trying to remember where here was. "I need information about a property." He handed Molly a slip of paper with the address of the building on E. 54th Street.

"What's this about?"

Randall couldn't maintain eye contact with Molly. "Better you don't know."

Molly reached for Randall's chin, gently but firmly turning his head until their eyes met. "Can I trust you?"

"It's me," Randall answered, as if that would be enough.

"I know." Molly wiped a tear from the corner of her eye. "Can I trust you?"

"I guess that's for you to decide."

They sat on the sofa in Molly's office. Neither said a word. Then Molly made her decision. She stood up from the sofa and moved to her desk.

"Let me see." She pulled up a file on her computer screen and scrolled through a long list of addresses.

"It's not one of ours."

"It used to be."

"What makes you think so?" Molly eyed Randall closely, looking for a tell.

"I read the archived file."

"I don't want to know." Molly turned her attention back to the computer screen. Randall waited while she sorted through old records. "Will you look at that! We managed the building until 2005."

"What can you tell me about it?"

"If you've seen the file, then you know everything that I do." She didn't want to get involved, but, hard as it was to admit, Molly still had a soft spot for Randall. "Are you in some kind of trouble?"

Randall told her about the postcard, the carnivore, and the mysterious interrogation (he left out the part about Jasmine).

"Give me a couple of days."

"I may not have a couple of days."

"I'll do the best I can." Molly stood up. "Let me show you out."

"I can find my way."

"Company rules." Molly blushed. "It's good to see you Randall."

MONEY AND POWER

"Who do you like this year, the Jets or the Giants?"

Randall's doorman half-laughed, half-belched. "Really, Mr. Riggs." He started telling Randall why the Jets were going to have a huge bounce-back season with their new coach, but Randall wasn't listening. He walked down the hall to the cluster mailbox and checked for mail. He was relieved to find that he had received nothing but junk. His recent experience with the mysterious postcard had him questioning his quarantine rules. He tossed the junk in the recycling without bothering to set it aside for two days.

Randall's phone was buzzing before he got off the elevator. It was a text message from Molly. "I have news about the building."

Randall's fingers danced across the touchscreen. "Call me."

"I'm in the office."

"Is that a problem?"

"I don't know… Maybe… Yes."

Randall threw caution to the wind. "Then meet me."

"No."

"Please."

"No." Molly stood firm. "I'll call."

Randall let himself into his apartment and waited for the phone call.

Ten minutes later, the phone rang. He didn't need to check the phone before picking up. He had no doubt that it would be Molly.

"What took so long?"

"Is that any way to say hello?"

Randall knew better than to rush Molly. She would tell him what he wanted to know when she was ready. "How are you Molly? Are you having a nice day?"

"I had to wait for your father to step out."

"Was I right about the building?"

"We managed the project until 2005. Your father handled it personally."

"I didn't think my father handled anything personally."

"Your father never liked the operations side, less since his health is failing..."

Randall made a note of Molly's remark, but didn't interrupt her.

"... but that building meant something to him. I don't know what and I don't know why."

"But he let the building go?"

"Yes, he did." Molly paused. "I don't know any of the details."

"Do you know who owns it now?"

"Listen to me Randall. Riggs & Son has been involved with that building since your grandfather's time. Talk to your father. He'll know more than I do." She didn't give Randall time to object. "Besides, I don't know how many more chances you'll have to make things right with your father. He's not a young man anymore."

"I don't know."

"If you're really in trouble, let your father help."

"I can't Molly.... I won't."

Molly heard something in Randall's tone that no one else could have heard. "If you're really in trouble, let your father help."

Molly knew him better than he knew himself. "I'll leave your father a note, letting him know that you'll be calling."

"I don't know."

"Too late Randall, I've written the note."

"I don't know."

"Too late, I hit send." Molly hung up the phone.

Randall pondered the essential question. Which was worse? To be interrogated in a nearly vacant office building by some unidentified government agent about a murder he knew nothing about or to have drinks with his father at the club?

***

Randall wondered whether he was in his father's phone. Would his name pop up on his father's screen? Would his father take the call or would he let it go to voicemail? Randall couldn't decide which outcome he was hoping for. He punched in the number and waited. And just like that, after too many years, he heard his father's voice. Randall was surprised. The voice didn't have the strength he once found so frightening.

"This is a surprise," his father said, by way of greeting.

"Molly told you I'd be calling."

"Yes, she did. She told me you needed my help." Randall Sr. paused. "You must be in a heap of trouble to reach out to your father."

"I need information about one of your buildings. Did Molly give you the address?"

"She did."

Randall wasn't sure how much to tell his father. "A woman died in the bar."

Randall Sr. measured his words carefully. "What is your connection to the dead woman?"

"There is none. At least, none that I know of." Randall Jr. laughed nervously. "The authorities believe that I know something... and I don't know why."

"Can you meet me at the club today?"

Randall Jr. despised the club and everything it represented. "What time?"

"I'm taking a steam at 3:00. Let's say 4:00."

***

Growing up, Randall hated when his father made him go to the club. The place smelled like money and power, whiskey, and cigars, and just a little bit like rat droppings. Jackets were required... even for the ten year-old son of a member.

It was always the same. They would start in the steam room. The fat old men wrapped in their Turkish towels made him uncomfortable. Even worse were the fat old men without their Turkish towels. Randall Jr. never knew where to look. He hid, as best he could, in the steam.

Then his father would take a massage from a swarthy man in white slacks and tee shirt. It was not always the same man, but it could have been. They all looked the same – swarthy, barrel-chested men with huge hands and Eastern European accents. Randall was scared of the swarthy men with white slacks and tee shirt. He was scared of their barrel-chests and huge hands.

After his father's massage, they would repair to the lounge. Randall Sr. would sip port and hail members from across the room, like they were ships at sea and he was the harbor master. He felt abandoned in the lounge, a small ship lost at sea, until he turned fourteen and started sneaking sips from poorly-attended whiskey glasses.

At 4:00, Randall Jr. walked into the club. It still smelled of money and power. It still smelled of whiskey and cigars. But it no longer smelled even a little bit like rat droppings. Apparently, in the intervening years, the club had solved its rat problem.

He made his way to the lounge and ordered a scotch on the rocks, on his father's account. He was sipping contentedly when his father hobbled into the room. Randall Jr. was stunned. Molly had warned him, but he was not ready for the old man who had at one time been his father. The man that he remembered was always impeccably dressed, a tall man with ramrod stiff posture. He was a man who needed no assistance and would brook no offers of same. In Randall's mind, his father was impervious to the passage of time. The man who hobbled into the lounge was stoop-shouldered, a shrunken man inside an oversized sport coat, dragging a bad leg behind him. A staff member kept a loose hand on Sr.'s upper arm as the man walked.

"Hello son."

Without waiting to be asked, staff brought Sr. a small glass of port.

"It's good to see you father." Randall saw the doubt on Sr.'s face. "Really."

"It's good to see you too, son."

Randall Jr. sipped his scotch. Sr. sipped his port. "Tell me everything."

Randall held back nothing. He told him about the postcard. About the bizarre interrogation. The implied threat. The newspaper account. He told him about everything except Jasmine.

Randall Sr. pulled a piece of notepaper from his jacket pocket. "Your grandfather bought the building in 1931. As the city came out of the depression, Edmund made a lot of money. It's fair to say that building helped launch Riggs & Son."

Perhaps for the first time, Randall Sr. regretted that he had not tried hard enough to involve his son in the family business. "When I was a boy, my father used to tell me stories about the Great Depression and how it jumpstarted his business empire. Did I ever tell you those stories?"

"Molly told me you personally managed the building."

Randall Sr. had to think for a moment. "That's true. We held onto the building for more than seventy years. But there came a time when it just made more sense to sell. We got an offer, what's that expression, they made us an offer we couldn't refuse. I lost track of the building since we let it go, but I recently learned that it may be available. Maybe I'm being sentimental, but I've entered into conversations to buy it back."

"With all due respect father, I don't picture you being swayed by sentiment."

"With good reason." Sr. laughed so hard, he snorted into his port. "Still, I'm interested. I think that Riggs & Son can survive one sentimental investment."

Randall signaled to the staff. One of the bartenders brought him another port. The bartender looked at Jr. "And you sir?"

Randall looked at his glass, nothing left but melting ice. "I guess I'll have one more."

When the bartender left, Randall Jr. asked about the dead body. "According to the records we found, the dead woman was in possession of a folder of real estate documents about the building on E. 54th St."

"I'm sorry son. I made a few calls, but I didn't learn anything useful, anything that is, except that my most trusted sources have all retired." Randall Sr. paused, deep in thought. "I'm getting too old for this."

"You're still a young man."

"I'm afraid not." He sipped his port. "So you spoke to Molly."

"Yes. It wasn't as uncomfortable as I thought it would be." He swallowed the last of his scotch. "For what it's worth, neither is this."

"I thought she was over you."

"She was." He paused. "To be clear, she still is."

"There was a time I thought she would give me grandchildren." Randall Sr. pulled out a handkerchief and wiped his eyes.

"Let's not do this again."

"Is it too much to ask for, that I should have a grandchild before I die?"

"It's not that simple." Randall replayed his father's words in his head. "Anyway, you're not dying."

"I'm not living."

Randall made a point of looking at his phone. "It's getting late. I need to leave." He stood. "Perhaps we can do this again."

Sr. looked up, surprise written all over his face. "You'd do that?"

Even though he was the one who made the offer, Randall was just as surprised as his father. "Yes. I think I would."

"Maybe next time, I can tell you stories about the early days at Riggs & Son."

"Maybe you can."

Randall Sr. grinned. "And we can take a steam?"

"I don't think so."

"You don't know what you're missing." Randall Sr. struggled to steady himself. "Here, help me up. I'll walk you to the door."

A RABBIT HOLE

"Last time we were here, Aadhik shared with us some valuable information about our little problem. We don't know who the dead woman is, or why someone wanted to kill her. But she was carrying a packet of documents about the building on E. 54th Street, so that might be important. We don't know how that author knows so much about the six of us, or how he figures into the mystery. But we do know where the woman died and we know when." Tony looked at the three other men and two women who were sitting in high back chairs, at the mahogany table in his conference room, drinking bitter coffee and sharing potentially useful information.

Jasmine spoke up. "I think I know who she is. Who she was."

Randall looked at Jasmine, surprise written on his face, but said nothing and waited for her to continue.

"Do any of you listen to podcasts?"

None of the men responded to Jasmine's question.

"The autopsy photo was nasty, but when Aadhik showed it to us, well, her red hair seemed vaguely familiar. So I did a little research of my own. The dead woman is Cecily Stephens. She does a weekly podcast about the sordid past of historic buildings." Jasmine shook her head. "I mean, she did a weekly podcast."

Cooper was skeptical. "Surely that bar isn't historical."

"Maybe, maybe not. The building has been around for more than a century." Jasmine sat back in the high back chair. "By the way, she hasn't done a new podcast this month."

"Okay then. We know more than we thought we did. We know who she was, we know where and when she died. We also know how she died. We've made a lot of progress, but we still don't know who killed her or why. And we don't know why the authorities believe we're involved." Tony looked around the conference table. "If you haven't already taken care of it, I would suggest you start working on your alibis."

Cooper jumped in. "I was watching college football."

"Can anyone confirm that?"

Cooper grinned. "I was on the phone with my bookie most of the day."

Jasmine smiled. "I was at the dumpling shop with my prayer group."

One by one, they went around the room. Each of them had an alibi. Bonnie was teaching a class at the local community center. Tony was at a charity golf event. Aadhik spent the day with his in-laws. Each of them had an alibi. Until they came to Randall. "I don't know. Maybe." He re-checked the calendar on his phone, as if this time, he would find some reminder as to how he had spent the day in question. "I'll figure something out."

"Please do," Tony replied. "I don't know why, but I have an uneasy feeling that if the authorities can implicate any one of us, they will manage to build a case against all of us."

Aadhik stood up to speak. "I spent all day yesterday at the Hall of Records."

"Thank you Aadhik. Did you learn anything?"

Aadhik blushed. I may have gone down a rabbit hole."

Jasmine interrupted. "What do you mean, down a rabbit hole?"

Aadhik made a face, thinking back on his day in the stacks. "You know how you start with good intentions, following the clues, but then something interesting grabs your attention, and you're pulled just a little bit off course, but then there's another grabber, and another, and before you know it, you've lost the purpose for your research and instead you've spent the day reading about an unsolved murder from 1931."

Tony shook his head. "Is there a point to any of this?"

"Probably not." Aadhik grinned. "Still isn't it odd that ninety years ago, the same building was at the center of one of the hottest murder trials in the city?"

Tony looked up, startled by Aadhik's remark. "Do I understand you to mean there was a woman murdered at Papillon back in 1931?"

"It wasn't Papillon back then. But it was a bar, and it was the scene of a sensational murder."

Randall had nearly nodded off when Aadhik started to talk about a rabbit hole. The mention of the building pulled him back in. "That's quite a coincidence."

Aadhik stared at Randall. "The case is full of coincidences. The building was owned by two partners. One of them was a man named Edmund Riggs, who went on to become a successful real estate developer. You're not descended from Edmund Riggs are you?"

"I should be so lucky." Randall chuckled at the idea. "Do I look like the scion of a business empire?"

Randall could feel all eyes on him.

Jasmine answered for the group. "No. Of course not." Still, she reminded herself, the veil that separates reality and illusion is as thin as her silk khata. "Please Aadhik, go on with your story."

"As I was saying, I'm sure it has nothing to do with our little mystery, but the Starlet Murder – that's what they called it in the tabloids – anyway, the Starlet Murder was a big story in 1931." Aadhik looked around the table. "According to the newspaper accounts, there were two men... partners in a budding business enterprise. Not only business partners, but they were also brothers-in-law, Edmund Riggs having married his partner's sister, Goldie."

Aadhik looked out the window. Rain obscured the view of the avenue, below. He turned back to the three men and two women who were waiting for him to finish his account of the Starlet Murder.

"After a long day's work, it was the custom of the business partners to repair to a local bar before heading home. With the influx of immigrants into the city, distinct neighborhoods emerged, each with their own traditions. Mostly, people stayed within their own neighborhood, but Edmund reportedly had a bit of a wild side. The two men became regulars at a small middle-eastern bar. It appears that they went, at first, for the arak, but returned, weekly, for the starlet."

"It seems that the bar owner's daughter had dreams of becoming a stage actress. By all accounts, she was well on her way. It was only a matter of time before she would find herself on Broadway." Aadhik checked his notes. "At least, that was the plan."

The story had nothing to do with their current problem, but they wanted to hear more.

"There's not much more to tell," Aadhik explained. "The newspaper accounts are sketchy, but there came a time when Edmund's partner – Sam – came to believe that Edmund was consorting with the starlet. When the starlet gave birth to a baby girl, Sam could not abide the dishonor that Edmund had brought on his sister.

"From that day forward, the two men could no longer be drinking partners. But business was business, so they tried as best they could to carry on. Then, according to the tabloids, there came a day when the bar owner discovered his daughter, the aspiring actress, dead on the bar room floor, an empty bottle of arak and two glasses on the polished wooden bar top.

"The police investigation, at first, focused on various middle-eastern men, swarthy men, with barrel-chests and huge hands. The police weren't overly concerned by the lack of any credible evidence tying their suspects to the crime. But Edmund was certain that his business partner had taken the life of the starlet as revenge against him. Edmund pushed the police to take action. Sam was arrested and subsequently indicted for the murder of the starlet. By the way..." Aadhik added, "... it's curious but in all the newspaper accounts, the young woman is never mentioned by name. She is just referred to as the starlet, or the consort, or sometimes as the corpse. The trial captured the imagination of the American public. The case was covered by many of the country's notable reporters."

"Was Sam found guilty?"

"After a long and contentious trial, the jury was unable to come to a unanimous decision."

Randall was fascinated by this unexpected bit of family history. "You said that Sam came to believe that Edmund was cheating. Was he?"

"Does that matter?"

"No, I guess not." Randall shook his head. "So what ever became of the baby?"

"I'm afraid her fate has been lost to the memories of men."

Aadhik took a sip of water and looked around the conference table. "Of course, that has nothing to do with our own troubles."

GREAT ELMS

Something about the Starlet Murder tugged at Jasmine's unconscious mind. She left Tony's conference room, and returned, straightaway to her apartment. She opened up her wooden cabinet and lit a stick of sandalwood incense. She removed the offering bowl, and offered up a brief prayer to the Buddha, as well as a flower she had found on the subway. Then she chanted.

The ritual always brought her a sense of cleansing renewal and this time was no exception, except she still felt the presence of the unanswered question. What was her unconscious mind trying to tell her? And why was she reminded of home?

Some problems are resolved by prayer and some by action, but the most important problems are often solved by sleep. Jasmine had long ago learned to trust her sleeping mind...

... Jasmine was strolling through a quiet little town. The town was home, or might have been, in another life. The street was lined with birch trees.

Jasmine knew that birch is a tree of protection. A birch-lined street is a good omen, and those who live on such streets are blessed with good health and special wisdom. She admired the tiny houses, with their flat roof and Bauhaus design. She wished she could knock on a door. She wondered who she would find inside. She had no time for that. And yet, she had all the time in the world.

She continued walking until she came to a small park, lined with elm trees, in the center of town. Great elms are dream trees. If she stepped into the park, Jasmine knew that she would be entering a dream within a dream. Or perhaps a nightmare. This was not the time to be timid. There is no yin without yang, she told herself. Jasmine measured her breathing and passed under the elm trees. She found herself on a well-worn path that bordered a lovely little meadow. A few feet ahead, or perhaps a few miles (what is distance anyway except illusion) Jasmine spotted a woman of indeterminate age, dressed in a purple robe and sporting orange running shoes, sitting on a park bench. The woman looked familiar, in the way that strangers often do.

"You're late," she said.

Jasmine wanted to ask the woman a question, but she had misplaced her voice. There was so much that she wanted to know, so much that this woman could tell her, but how could Jasmine ask without a voice?

The woman nodded her head and smiled. "Look in your pocket."

Jasmine reached into her pocket and pulled out her voice. "Who are you?"

"I am Madame Alexina. I am responsible for this place." She paused. "You may call me Alex."

"I'm lost. Can you help me find my way?"

Madame Alexina stared into Jasmine's eyes. "You already know the way."

Jasmine protested, but Madame Alexina was adamant. "Use the password."

"But I don't know the password!"

"You must conjure one up."

"I don't know how."

"Then I can't help you."

Jasmine despaired of finding her way. If Madame Alexina couldn't help her, then what was she to do? A soft wind began to blow, rustling through the trees. Jasmine listened to the trees. She leaned over and whispered the password in Madame Alexina's ear. "Jabberwocky."

Madame Alexina nodded approvingly. From under her purple robe, she pulled out a glowing orb and handed it to Jasmine. "The orb will lead you where you need to go."

Jasmine felt the orb slowly come to life in her hands. It was as if the orb was breathing. She put one foot in front of the other, trusting the orb to guide her through the park. She enjoyed the majesty of the great elms and the serenity of the meadow. She gave herself over to the orb as it pulsated in her hands. As she walked, she could sense the orb's breathing quicken. She was confident that she was approaching the "Center."

***

Jasmine woke early, and reached for the glowing orb. In the light of day, she was forced to admit, it was, at best, a dream orb, unavailable to her in this world. When she reached for the orb, her hand closed on the remote.

Jasmine turned on the TV, just the picture, no sound. With the sound muted, it was mostly just talking heads, but it helped pass the time. Then a clip came on the screen. The author.

She watched the silent news clip, growing increasingly anxious. She turned up the volume and listened as the author chatted about the murder of Cecily Stephens. A chill went down her spine.

Jasmine opened the wooden cabinet in her studio apartment. She lit a stick of sandalwood incense and brewed a small pot of tea. She said a brief prayer before the statue of the Buddha, but peace eluded her.

The police investigation was ongoing. How did the author know so much?

ONE STIPULATION

Randall took a sip of cheap red wine. Before it reached his stomach, he could feel the wine coming back up. He grabbed the cloth napkin and held it over his mouth. Randall struggled to gain control of his gag reflex. After a brief, but dangerous moment, he put the napkin down and breathed in deeply. "That's horrid." Randall took a sip of water and examined the label on the wine bottle. "How did we ever drink that?"

"We were kids. What did we know?" Molly looked at him from across the table.

"I knew I wanted to be with you."

"And I wanted to be with you." Molly didn't know what else to say. "Until wanting to be with you wasn't good enough anymore."

Randall signaled for the waiter. "Please remove this swill and bring us a nice Bordeaux."

Molly reached for the breadbasket, busying herself with the choice of fresh-baked rolls. After making her selection, she passed the basket to Randall.

"I didn't think you would join me for lunch today." He smiled. "Especially on such short notice."

Before Molly could respond, the waiter returned with a 2015 Bordeaux and two goblets. "I figured you'd want clean glasses," the waiter explained.

Molly waited while Randall tasted the Bordeaux. The waiter poured the wine and departed. When they were alone, Molly resumed the conversation. "I figured if you and your father could repair your relationship, maybe we could too."

Randall nodded his head. "I'd like that."

"I would too," Molly said. "It sounds like you had a good visit with your father."

"What did he tell you?"

"Only that he was glad to see you and that he looked forward to doing it again."

"Yes, that sums it up pretty well." Randall thought back on their chat at the club. "Except I was surprised to see how frail he was."

"It's been a long time since you saw your father. Time has not been good to him."

"What do his doctors say? What's wrong with him?"

"Nothing's wrong with him, Randall. Nothing, except he's an old man with nothing to live for."

"He's not that old."

"Old is more than just a number, Randall." Molly smiled. "I'm glad you reached out to him."

Randall nodded his head in agreement. "I guess I am too."

Their conversation was interrupted by the arrival of their antipasto platter. Randall picked at a few olives and artichoke hearts. Molly went straight for the mozzarella.

Between bites, Randall and Molly made small talk. Both of them understood that the serious conversations could wait.

The waiter returned with their entrees – one fettucine Bolognese and one lunch salad. Randall picked at his salad. Molly ate all the Bolognese, except for a bit she spilled on the tablecloth.

She studied Randall's face. It was the face she remembered, only it had more depth to it now. "I guess your father isn't the only one getting older. There are days I cringe at the idea that I'm not a kid anymore."

"We've wasted a lot of years." Randall knew he was making a mistake, but he couldn't shove the words back into his mouth. "Years we could have spent together."

"No Randall. I'm sorry, we could not have spent those years together." Molly reached for her napkin and wiped a tear from her eye. "No matter how much I wanted to."

Molly segued from one uncomfortable topic to another. "How much trouble are you in?"

"I don't know." Randall catalogued his troubles. "A woman was murdered on October 2nd at the French bistro, Papillon. She died of a knife wound to the chest. For some reason, the authorities believe I was involved."

"That's terrible!" Molly didn't know much about how Randall had spent the last decade, but she was confident that murder wasn't any part of it. "Do they have anything incriminating?"

"I don't know. They're holding their cards close to the vest, so to speak."

"Is there anything I can do to help?"

Randall had been waiting for Molly to ask. Now that she had, he was uncomfortable with what he needed her to do. "You can help me with an alibi."

"What!"

"Look Molly, if I was guilty of something, you can be sure I'd be smart enough to arrange for an alibi. But I didn't kill the woman, didn't aid and abet whoever did, didn't have anything to do with it."

"I believe you." Molly felt sick to her stomach. "So just tell the authorities where you were. I'm sure someone can corroborate your story."

"That's the problem. I'm not sure what I did on the 2nd. There's nothing on my calendar. I may have spent the day alone in my apartment."

"You may have? What does that mean?"

Randall stared at the floor. "I think I began the day with a bottle of single malt. The rest of the day is a blur."

"You can't expect me to lie for you. I can't be your alibi." Molly excused herself and went in search of the ladies' room. Randall wondered if she was going to return. In the ladies' room, Molly was wondering the same thing. She had a decision to make.

When she did return, there were two cups of coffee on the table. Next to each cup was a biscotti. They finished the meal in silence.

Randall paid the bill. Lunch had started off so well and had come to such an uncomfortable end. "Can I hail you a cab?"

"Thank you." Molly stood up slowly. "If I'm asked, I'll tell the authorities you were with me when the woman was murdered."

"Thank you." Randall didn't know what else to say.

Molly had one stipulation.

"Except for your visit to Riggs & Son, I haven't seen you in more than a decade. If I'm going to be your alibi, it would be helpful if people saw us together now and then. Maybe even believed that we were an item."

"Are we..." Randall asked, "...an item?"

Molly threw her arms around Randall and kissed him in a way that was sure to draw the notice of the wait staff. "Of course not." She kissed him again. "except when we're around people who can confirm our itemhood to the authorities."

A HANDSOME GRANDSON

When Randall told his father that he would like to see him again, he hadn't meant right away, but he needed to learn more about the early days at Riggs & Son. So, after lunch with Molly, he went back to the club, and, to his very great surprise, he joined his father in the steam room. He wrapped himself in an enormous Turkish towel and draped a second towel over his head. He allowed his vision to blur in the steam. He would broach no social interaction in the steam room. Randall could feel the toxins draining from his body as he sweat.

Twenty minutes later, his father was ready for a massage and suggested that Randall take one as well.

Randall drew a line in the sand. "I'll freshen up and wait for you in the lounge."

Randall Sr. went off for his massage. Jr. took a cold shower, got dressed and went in search of his first whiskey of the day.

He was sitting in the lounge, chatting with the afternoon bartender when his father walked into the room. He was still moving slowly, but Randall noticed that his father's limp was noticeably improved. "Your leg doesn't seem to be bothering you so much today."

"Some days are better than others."

Randall Sr. waited for his port and then father and son moved to one of the small conversation nooks in the lounge. "I understand that you spoke to Molly."

"Yes."

"How was it?"

"We went to Luigi's. The food was excellent."

"That's not what I meant."

"I know that." Randall chuckled. "It was good."

"So you think you might see her again?"

"I think I might."

"One day, you and Molly are going to give me a handsome grandson, to carry on the family name."

The two men lapsed into silence, each contemplating a future that neither man believed.

"What can I do for you, son?"

"Tell me about Edmund, about the early days at Riggs & Son Royal Management."

Randall Sr. smiled. "Of course, in the beginning it wasn't Riggs & Son."

Randall nodded. "Of course, it was just Edmund... Riggs Royal Management."

"It wasn't just Edmund." After all these years, Randall Sr. was ready to tell his son the truth about the business. "In the beginning, Edmund had a partner. His name was Sam Royal. The company was Riggs & Royal Management."

"I'll be damned."

"There are some who say it was the business that was damned."

Randall Sr. sipped his port.

Jr. sipped his whiskey, allowing his father to tell the story in his own way. There were parts of the story that Randall knew and parts that he suspected, but he needed to hear all of it, and hear it from his father.

Before Randall Sr. could continue, the club manager came over to speak to Sr. "I'm sorry to bother you, sir, but there seems to be a problem." The club manager looked toward the lobby. Randall Jr. followed his gaze. Tony, Aadhik, Jasmine, Cooper and Bonnie were standing just inside the front entrance. They were quite a group – Tony in his brightly colored sweater, Aadhik with his suit and silk paisley tie, Cooper wearing his golf shirt with the insignia on the pocket, Bonnie sporting her Harvard cap, and of course Jasmine, in her yellow hippie dress. "Are you expecting guests? We don't have them on your list."

Randall Jr. jumped in before his father had time to respond. "I'm sorry. They're with me. I should have told you."

The club manager smiled indulgently. "As pleased as we are that you have come to see your father, I'm sure you understand that you don't have the authority to invite guests."

"I know, but..." Randall Jr. turned to his father.

Sr. frowned. "The history of Riggs & Son is a private matter. Even if I were inclined to meet your friends, this is neither the time nor the place."

"You don't understand. They're involved. They have a right to hear this."

Randall Sr. instructed the club manager to set up a small table for his guests. When they were all seated, and introductions made, Randall Sr. picked up where he had left off.

"By all accounts Edmund & Sam were good friends and even better partners. Edmund managed the business side. Sam was the people person. When Edmund revealed to his business partner that he wanted to meet a woman he could start a family with, Sam introduced him to his sister Goldie."

"Grandma Goldie?"

"That's right. Your Grandma died much too young; God rest her soul."

"Tell me about her."

Randall Sr. grew wistful. "I was only a child when she died. "What I know comes from neighborhood gossip and from the rag sheets. It was not something a young boy could ask his father."

Randall waited for his father to continue.

"Edmund and Goldie loved each other very much, but after I was born, and the business began to grow, Edmund focused on the business. Goldie focused on raising her infant son. The story, as I heard it (and I don't know if it's true) was that my father had a brief affair with a young actress. The affair resulted in a bastard child. Sam couldn't abide the dishonor Edmund had done to his sister Goldie."

Randall Sr. signaled for another port. When the port arrived, Sr. took a sip and resumed his tale.

"The starlet was murdered, a knife wound to her chest. She bled out on the bar room floor. Newspaper accounts are contradictory as to witnesses. One paper reported that the bar was empty at the time of the knifing. Another paper claimed the bar was packed with customers, but that no one paid attention to the starlet, dead on the bar room floor."

"The police arrested Sam. In court, the prosecuting attorney argued that Sam had killed the woman to punish Edmund for his infidelity. Six of the jurors voted to convict. Six voted not guilty."

"What happened?"

"The prosecuting attorney decided not to retry the case." Randall Sr. forced himself to finish the story. "Two weeks later, Sam was found dead in their office. No one was charged in the murder."

"But surely you have an opinion."

Randall Sr. had spent a lifetime hiding from his opinion. "I think Edmund was a sonofabitch."

It looked to Randall like a weight had suddenly been lifted off his father's shoulders. He sat up straight in the chair, his shoulders squared, with that ramrod stiff posture that Randall remembered. "There is something I don't understand."

"Only one thing," his father replied. "Then you're doing better than I am."

"There's nothing in that building anymore except for painful memories. Why do you want to buy it?"

"I don't think I knew until this very moment. Or to be more accurate, I think I always knew, but couldn't say the words. I want to demolish the building. I want to eliminate any evidence that it ever existed." Randall Sr. frowned. "I don't want a century-old double murder to be my future grandson's legacy."

FRIENDS WITH BENEFITS

Randall climbed out of a cab in front of his apartment. The doorman held the door open. "Good afternoon, Mr. Riggs."

"How are you doing today?"

"Not as good as you sir."

Randall was already moving through the lobby, heading for the cluster mailboxes. He turned back, glancing at the doorman. "Huh."

The doorman stammered. "Your new girlfriend, sir" but Randall wasn't listening. He was opening his mailbox and sorting through the day's junk.

He took the elevator to his apartment on the fifth floor. When he opened the apartment door, Molly was standing in his kitchen, the refrigerator door wide open. "Do you have anything to eat in here?"

"How did you get in?"

Molly laughed. "The doorman and I have an understanding."

"An understanding?"

"I explained it to you at Luigi's. If you expect your alibi to stand up, people have to believe that we're a couple."

"You said we would be an item in public. My apartment isn't public."

"Don't you like coming home and finding me here to greet you." Molly pouted. "I thought that's what you wanted."

"You're right. I've wanted that ever since you broke up with me. Now I'm not so sure." Randall shrugged. "I mean, it's fun to pretend, but I'm not that kid any more. Neither are you."

"That's true." Molly found a plain yogurt in the back of the refrigerator. She grabbed a banana off the kitchen counter, cut it up and blended it into the yogurt. "This'll do."

Randall grinned. "Perhaps, after all this time, we can just be friends. What do you say?"

"Maybe friends with benefits?" Molly kissed him on the cheek.

Randall didn't know what to say, so he said nothing at all.

"How was your visit with your father?"

"It was good. He even convinced me to take a steam."

Molly laughed. "I don't believe it!"

"Really."

Molly grew serious. "Have you heard anything more about the investigation?"

"When I was questioned, the carnivore – that's what I call him – anyway, the carnivore told me not to leave town. He made it clear that he would be in touch." Randall rubbed his chin. "I keep expecting to hear something."

"Did your father learn anything that could be helpful?" Molly seemed particularly interested in what Randall Sr. did or didn't know.

"We talked about the early days at Riggs & Son. Did you know when it started, Edmund had a business partner?"

Before Molly could respond, Randall's cell phone shrieked from across the room. Randall retrieved the phone. "Hello." He walked into the bedroom to take the call. He had spent the last few days preparing for the phone call, but still, he wasn't ready.

The carnivore kept it brief. "We have some unfinished business to attend to. Come to my office, tomorrow at noon."

"Yes. I understand. Tomorrow at noon."

He barely had time to end the call, before the texts started arriving... from Tony, from Aadhik, from Cooper and Bonnie, and, of course, from Jasmine. Obviously they had all received the same phone call. Jasmine's text was clear. "We're on our way over to your apartment. We need to talk."

Randall texted back. "We?" But Jasmine didn't respond.

Randall walked back into the kitchen. "The shit is about to hit the proverbial fan."

"What shit?"

Randall wondered whether he meant the next day's meeting with the carnivore or Jasmine's impending arrival.

Fifteen minutes later, there was a knock on the door. Randall assumed it was Jasmine, but when he opened the door, it was Cooper and Bonnie who were standing in the doorway.

"Thanks for letting us meet here." Cooper looked around the apartment, checking out, first, the fireplace, and second, Molly. "Nice."

Bonnie went straight for the refrigerator and grabbed a bottle of white wine.

Before Randall could say anything, there was another knock on the door. Randall looked over at Molly. "Could you get that?"

When Molly opened the door, she found Jasmine standing in the hallway. Jasmine was startled by the unfamiliar woman in Randall's apartment. "Who the hell are you?"

Randall hurried over. "Molly, this is Jasmine. Jasmine, Molly." He didn't have time for explanations, he didn't even have time to shut the apartment door before he spotted Tony and Aadhik getting off the elevator and looking for the apartment.

Tony was out of breath. His face was as bright as his sweater. He started asking questions as soon as he reached the apartment door. "Did any of you send me a video?"

Randall was confused. "A video? No."

"Anybody?" Tony searched their faces, but all he got back were blank stares.

"Did any of you receive the video?" Tony was obviously distraught. "Am I the only one?"

Bonnie poured Tony a small glass of white wine. “Take a swallow. Then tell us what you’re talking about.”

Tony allowed himself a sip. “I was on the way over here, when this showed up on my phone.”

Tony showed them the video message. It was a short clip, but damning. It showed the six of them, leaving the crime scene, stepping over the dead body.

“That’s not us! It can’t be!”

“What the hell is going on here?”

“That’s crazy!”

They were all of them talking all at once, and all at the top of their lungs.

Jasmine quietly began to chant. “Nam-myoho-renge-kyo. Nam-myoho-renge-kyo.”

Soon, they were all chanting. “Nam myoho renge-kyo.”

After a few minutes, they were able to talk.

Cooper looked around the room. “It’s a doctored tape. It has to be.”

Bonnie nodded her head. “Of course it’s a doctored tape. But can we prove it?”

No one had an answer.

Jasmine steadied her breathing. “All we can do is tell the truth.”

Randall was skeptical. “Will that be enough?”

A faint smile struggled to find purchase on Jasmine’s face. “It will have to be.”

Bonnie, Cooper and Aadhik nodded their heads in agreement.

Randall shrugged.

Jasmine stared at Molly. "Can we talk in front of... her?"

Molly walked over to Randall and gave him a kiss. "Go ahead and talk with your friends, sweetheart. I can wait in the bedroom."

Randall looked from Jasmine to Molly and then back to Jasmine. "Molly is my girlfriend. There are no secrets between us."

Jasmine still wasn't sure if it was safe to speak in front of Molly. She started off cautiously. "Someone is trying to shake us up before tomorrow's interrogation. I don't know about the rest of you, but I'd like to avoid any more surprises."

Bonnie looked around the room. "I think that's a good idea. I have no intention of going down for something I wasn't involved in."

Cooper nodded his head in agreement. "Something that none of us were involved in... no matter what the video suggests."

"Yes, of course," replied Tony. "We're in this together."

Randall spoke up. "The first time we met the carnivore, he accused us of playing a part in a murder that we knew nothing about. This time we'll be better prepared. After all, we know a lot about the case. If we tell him what we know, we should be fine."

Tony watched Randall closely. "So what do we know for sure?"

Aadhik, as usual, stood up to speak. "We know a woman was murdered in Papillon on E. 54th Street, on or about October 2."

Jasmine nodded. "Her name was Cecily Stephens."

They ran through everything else they knew – the where, the when and the how of the murder. They couldn't decide about the Starlet Murder. It didn't seem to have anything to do with the death of Cecily Stephens, but there were too many coincidences to dismiss it entirely.

Tony looked at Randall. "When Aadhik asked you if you were descended from Riggs money, you said no."

Randall looked down at the floor. "I did."

"That was a lie."

"It was."

"Would you like to explain?"

"My father and I don't get along. Until this week, I hadn't seen him in ten years. It didn't seem…"

While Tony and Randall spoke, Bonnie had been checking something on her cellphone. She interrupted with a news flash. "Randall, turn on your television."

"Huh?"

"Your television." Bonnie located the remote and did it herself.

A newsman was interviewing the author. In the background, there was a picture of the book cover. By the time they looked over at the TV, the reporter was cutting to commercial.

After the commercial break, the newsman moved on to another story.

"Damn, we missed it." Cooper turned to Bonnie. "What did he say?"

"I missed most of it." Bonnie paused. "Anyway, that's not our problem. Our problem is October 2."

Tony added, "At least we all have alibis. Once he checks our alibis, the agent will realize we have no part in the crime. I was at a golf outing." He looked at the other members in the gang of six, studying their faces for any sign of trouble. "Am I right, that we do all have alibis?"

Jasmine jumped in. "I was with my prayer group at the dumpling shop."

Cooper nodded. "I was on the phone with my bookie."

They went around the room, confirming that they could all account for their whereabouts on the date of the murder.

Bonnie reminded them that she had been teaching a class at the community center.

Aadhik stood up. "I was with my in-laws."

Finally it was Randall's turn. Jasmine watched him closely. Randall couldn't return the gaze. He looked up at the ceiling. "I was with Molly."

Molly looked right at Jasmine. "We spent the entire day in bed."

Randall's face turned bright red. "No one needs to hear that."

Tony tried to deflect the tension in the apartment. "Well anyway, we all have an alibi."

Bonnie wasn't satisfied. "I'd feel better walking into the interrogation tomorrow if we knew why the woman was murdered."

Jasmine offered up her best guess. "Ms. Stephens was a podcaster. She reported on the sordid past of some of the city's most iconic buildings. She must have pissed off a lot of people along the way."

Aadhik pulled a sheaf of papers from his pocket and rifled through them. "You may be right. But we don't know who was pissed off enough to commit murder."

Tony had heard enough. "It's not our job to solve the crime. Only to clear our names." He looked around the room and smiled. "I think we've done that. Don't you?"

Everyone quickly agreed.

There didn't seem to be much point in continuing the conversation. They knew what they knew. Hopefully, it would be enough. It would have to be. One by one, they said their goodbyes.

Finally, it was just Jasmine, Molly and Randall. Randall turned to Molly. "Could you give us a moment alone? I need to talk to Jasmine."

All Jasmine wanted was to leave. "That won't be necessary. You don't owe me an explanation, Randall."

"Please." Randall looked at Molly, then Jasmine, then back at Molly.

"I'll wait in the bedroom."

Randall waited until Molly was in the bedroom. He made sure the door was shut tight.

"It's not what it looks like."

"It's exactly what it looks like." Jasmine laughed nervously. "It's just you never mentioned a girlfriend. I shouldn't be here."

"Please, sit down. It's important to me that you understand."

Jasmine sat down and waited for the explanation. She hoped that Randall would just be honest with her, and apologize for leading her on.

"Molly works for my father. I've known her since college."

And that's supposed to make me feel better?

"Ten years ago, she was my girlfriend. Ten years ago."

"Then what was this," and she waved around the apartment, "all about? Why the charade?"

"I needed an alibi. The truth is I drank too much and don't remember what I was doing on the 2nd. Molly offered to be my alibi."

"Okay. I guess that makes sense, but.."

"Molly said my story would hold up better if people believed that we really were a couple."

"So you're not a couple."

"No."

Jasmine kissed Randall on the cheek. "Just to be clear, we're not a couple either."

Randall grinned. "We could be."

"One thing at a time." Jasmine kissed him again. "First, there's the small matter of a murder to deal with."

A SWEET STORY

The first time they had been summoned by the carnivore, they had arrived alone, six separate individuals, each with their own personal story. But following the interrogation, the challenge to clear their names had bound them together. They agreed to return to the building as a team, all for one and one for all, the "gang of six." They would sink or swim as one. They met early in the morning, in front of Tony's office and walked to the meeting.

In a matter of days, they had learned much about the murder, and also about one another. Perhaps they didn't know everything, but they knew quite a lot. They could all account for their whereabouts on the day that Cecily Stephens had been murdered. The sun was shining. There was a bounce in their step.

"We've got this," Tony said.

Randall agreed. They did have this. Only there was a nagging doubt in the back of his head, like a low-pressure headache. Randall shook it off. "Yeah, we've got this."

The four men and two women stood in front of the building. They were eager to get this over with, but perhaps, here at the last, they each needed a moment, lost in their own thoughts, and perhaps, in each other's.

Jasmine pushed the button. There was a buzz and a bit of static. They had gained entrance.

"Let's go."

They checked the building directory and made their way to the carnivore's office. They were surprised to see a large man standing behind the reception desk. He looked like a refrigerator in a gray pinstripe suit.

"Please, take a seat. He will be ready for you shortly."

The meetings in Tony's conference room had established their regular seating arrangement. Randall took his "assigned" seat at the table. Jasmine, Tony, Cooper, Bonnie and Aadhik did the same.

Randall wondered if he could ask for a cup of coffee. He looked over at the "receptionist" and decided against making the request.

The office door opened. In walked the carnivore. "Good. You're all here on time. Let's get started."

He pulled up a chair and joined them at the table. "Last time, we got nowhere. Let's hope that today's 'chat' is more productive." He reviewed his notes and smiled his carnivore smile.

"Now that I've got your attention... I'm the agent who gets to decide whether or not you get sent to the big show... whether you get what you deserve. So don't waste my time, don't feed me some line. I have no doubt that one of you had the lead role in this and all of you played some part."

No one said a word.

"I'm doing you a favor. Later you're going to have to answer to a higher authority." The carnivore paused. "So let's start over. Who knows why you're all here in my office?"

This time Randall had an answer. "There was a murder, and we're all suspects. But we've been doing our own investigation and we can explain everything. And don't forget, we're innocent until proven guilty."

"Who can tell me when this went down?"

Jasmine smiled innocently. "There's video footage of the killers leaving the scene two weeks ago, on October 2nd."

"Okay, where did it happen then?" The carnivore pointed at Cooper. "You!"

Cooper looked at the carnivore and smiled. "They found the body at the French Bistro Papillon."

"Okay. Tell me about the victim." The carnivore looked at Aadhik. "I want details."

This time, Aadhik was ready with an answer. "The victim was a woman named Cecily Stephens. She was a podcaster."

"What was she wearing?"

It was Bonnie's turn to speak. "She was wearing an expensive green dress."

"Did the victim have anything unusual? Money? Jewelry? Drugs?"

Tony filled in the details. "She had a folder filled with documents about the building on E. 54th, you know, the building that houses Papillon."

"That's better." The carnivore watched the gang of six closely "But you still need to account for your whereabouts when this was happening. The carnivore watched the gang of six closely. "Who wants to go first?"

Cooper jumped up. "In the fall, my Saturdays are devoted to college football. I was on the phone all day with my bookie."

They went around the room, each one accounting for their whereabouts. Bonnie told the carnivore about teaching a class at the community center. Aadhik talked about spending the day out-of-town with his in-laws. They went to a basketball game together. Tony explained about the charity golf outing. He even had a photograph of the foursome.

Jasmine spoke up. "I spent the day with my prayer group at the dumpling shop. I ate dumplings."

When it was Randall's turn, he explained that he had spent the day with his girlfriend. "I had too much to drink, but Molly can tell you that we spent the day together."

"If I call her in, I assume that she'll corroborate your story?"

"Of course." A nervous laugh slipped from Randall's pursed lips.

The carnivore stood up and walked around the room. "That's much better. Really. Much, much better." He went to the window and looked out on the street below. "Of course, we haven't talked about motivation. I don't need to tell you the importance of motivation." He paced around the room. "We're running out of time."

Jasmine had been pondering the question of motivation. If they knew why, she reasoned, they might also know who. "I think it has something to do with the building..." She trailed off.

"The building? What do you mean?"

"Cecily Stephens was a podcaster. She was murdered in Papillon while preparing to do a story about the building that houses the bar."

Aadhik stood up. "The Starlet Murder."

Aadhik's answer startled all of them, especially Randall. "What does a ninety year-old cold case have to do with Cecily's murder?"

Aadhik admitted that he didn't know, but Bonnie had an idea. "Someone didn't want her to tell that story. But who?"

Randall's heart was racing. Bonnie was correct. Someone didn't want the story to be told. Randall whispered something.

The carnivore turned in his direction. "Did you say something?"

Randall shook his head slowly. "I killed Cecily Stephens."

Stunned silence engulfed the room. No one knew what to say. Even the carnivore was silent. Finally Jasmine spoke up. "No Randall, you didn't."

"Yes, I did. I wanted to spare my father the embarrassment. I only wanted to scare her, but she wasn't willing to back off the story. Things got out of control. It was me. Just me."

Jasmine wasn't impressed by Randall's account. "No Randall. You didn't kill anyone. And you can't protect the person who did."

Jasmine persisted. “If you don’t tell them who killed Ms. Stephens, I will.”

Randall put his head in his heads. “Molly O’Sullivan killed Cecily Stephens.”

No one said a word. Finally, the carnivore spoke up. “Why would this O’Sullivan lady want to kill the podcaster?”

Randall slumped in his chair.

Jasmine spoke softly. “When Molly offered to be his alibi, Randall jumped at the chance. It didn’t occur to him, until just now, that it was actually Molly who needed the alibi.”

Randall raised his head off the table. “I thought she was helping me.”

Jasmine finished Randall’s thought for him. “When all the time, she was using you as her alibi.”

Tony spoke up for all of them, “Why would your girlfriend care about the Starlet Murder case?”

“Edmund was my great grandfather. It would have destroyed my father to have the true story of Riggs & Son plastered all over the internet.”

Everyone had the same doubts. Tony was the first to speak up. “That seems to point to you, Randall, not your girlfriend. What’s in it for her?”

“Molly has worked at Riggs & Son for ten years. She’s my father’s personal assistant. To be honest, he’s been more like a father to her than he ever was to me.”

The carnivore growled. “That’s a sweet story you’re spinning. Too bad it isn’t true.”

Randall said nothing. Jasmine spoke up. “Of course it’s true.”

The carnivore shared his own theory of the crime. "Randall Riggs Sr. is an old man, in poor health. When he dies, his son stands to inherit a fortune. Do you have any idea how much Riggs & Son is worth? Randall here stands to inherit a fortune. He had the means, the motive and the opportunity."

The carnivore sat back in his chair. "And he confessed."

Randall said nothing. Tony said nothing. Cooper, Bonnie and Aadhik said nothing. Jasmine began to chant.

The carnivore smiled. His teeth sparkled. "Randall Riggs Jr., you will be brought to trial on a charge of murder in the first degree. The rest of you will face indictment on the charge of accessory after the fact."

THE TRIAL

The district attorney fast tracked the trial. The gang of six had little opportunity to prepare a defense. Still, they were not overly concerned. Of course, anyone would be anxious, facing a murder charge, but they knew the real story. They knew the real killer. They were confident they would be acquitted on all counts.

Of course, that's not what happened. The prosecutor presented his theory of the crime. The defense attorney countered with his own version of the events. But, by all accounts, it was the prosecutor's closing argument that sealed Randall's fate.

"On October 2nd, a young woman, Cecily Stephens was stabbed by an assailant at a midtown bistro. The victim was a podcaster. She was well-known in real estate circles for reporting on the sordid history of iconic New York City buildings. She was working on a story that would have been harmful to the real estate company owned by the defendant's father. In cases like this, it is important to ask who stood to gain from Ms. Stephen's murder."

The prosecutor took a moment to make eye contact, one by one, with each member of the jury. "Some of you might believe that the defendant's father, Randall Riggs Sr is responsible for the death of Cecily Stephens, but the elder Mr. Riggs is an old man in poor health, incapable of the committing this heinous crime. Not even the defendant's own attorney has tried to suggest that we have charged the wrong member of the Riggs family. No, I think we can safely eliminate Randall Riggs Sr from the suspect list."

"Who does the defense offer up as the presumed murderer? The defendant's ex-girlfriend. Think about that. Molly O'Sullivan broke the defendant's heart. For the past ten years, the defendant has felt the wound from that break-up. It is reason enough for the defendant to implicate his ex-girlfriend in this sordid affair."

"And it is likely the cause of the defendant's excessive drinking. Let me remind you of his alcohol-induced memory lapses. The defendant wouldn't know the true story unless it came out of a bottle and was served to him on the rocks."

The prosecutor pointed to Molly sitting in the courtroom. "There is no actual evidence of any wrongdoing by this sweet woman, just a fanciful tale from a desperate, and well-paid defense attorney."

"I ask again, who stands to gain from Ms. Stephens murder? The real estate company, after all, is Riggs & Son. Randall Riggs Jr is the only person with the motive, the means, and the opportunity to take the life of Cecily Stephens. If that's not enough, I must remind you that the defendant confessed to the crime."

"Let me repeat myself. The defendant, Randall Riggs Jr confessed to the murder!"

Randall Riggs Jr. was found guilty of murder. He was sentenced to life, without parole. Tony, Jasmine, Aadhik, Cooper and Bonnie were convicted as accessories after the fact. They were each sentenced to twenty years, eligible for parole after twelve.

To this day, they maintain their innocence.

PUBLISHER'S NOTE

Recently we learned that Randall and the rest of the "gang of six" were not responsible for the murder of Cecily Stephens.

It is our understanding that lawyers are preparing the papers necessary to exonerate the gang of six. By the time you read this, it is our sincere hope that they will have been released from jail.

Randall, Jasmine, Tony, Aadhik, Bonnie and Cooper were the victims of an insidious plot hatched by an evil madman.

But we were just as much a victim as were the falsely imprisoned gang of six. We did not know that the author was lying when he wrote the book. We certainly did not know that the author himself was guilty of the cold-blooded murder of Cecily Stephens.

We did not know that the "bastard child" born of the affair between Edmund and the starlet was, in fact, the author's mother. The murdered starlet would have been his grandmother. By framing Randall for the murder of Cecily Stephens, the author was taking revenge on three generations of Riggs. His motives for framing Randall were deeply emotional, driven not by logic, but by hatred. It is evidence of the author's cold-blooded determination that he was willing to murder an innocent woman to bring about Randall's downfall.

Had we known the truth, we would not have published *Motive for Murder*. Now that the story is out, we believe it is our duty to keep this important book in print. If the gang of six names us in any lawsuit, we will make a vigorous defense.

ABOUT THE AUTHOR

Jeff Markowitz is the author of five mysteries, including three books in the Cassie O'Malley Mystery series and two standalone mysteries. Jeff introduced readers to tabloid reporter and amateur sleuth Cassie O'Malley in 2004, in *Who is Killing Doah's Deer*. Cassie returned in 2006 in *A Minor Case of Murder* and in 2009 in *It's Beginning to Look a Lot like Murder*. In 2015, his black comedy *Death and White Diamonds* won a Lovey Award and a David Award. *Hit or Miss*, released in 2020, was an Amazon Hot New Release in Political Fiction. Jeff is both the author of and a character in this novella, *Motive for Murder*.

Jeff spent more than forty years creating community-based programs, services and supports for children and adults with autism, before retiring in 2018 to devote more time to writing.

Jeff lives in Monmouth Junction NJ with his wife Carol and two cats Vergil and Aeneas. Jeff is Past President of the New York Chapter of Mystery Writers of America.

Jeff is currently on the lam.

Made in the USA
Middletown, DE
09 July 2023